Tyrannosaurus Ted

by Joan Stimson

Illustrated by Tomislav Zlatic

W
FRANKLIN WATTS

First published in 2009 by
Franklin Watts
338 Euston Road
London
NW1 3BH

Franklin Watts Australia
Level 17/207 Kent Street
Sydney
NSW 2000

A CIP catalogue record for this book is available from the British Library.

ISBN 978 0 7496 9187 5 (hbk)
ISBN 978 0 7496 9193 6 (pbk)

Series Editor: Jackie Hamley
Editor: Melanie Palmer
Series Advisor: Dr Barrie Wade
Series Designer: Peter Scoulding

Printed in China

Franklin Watts is a division of
Hachette Children's Books,
an Hachette UK company.
www.hachette.co.uk

There once was a
dinosaur called
Tyrannosaurus Ted.

But Ted didn't like to fight.

He liked to dance instead.

He danced in
the sunshine.

He danced beneath
the moon.

And always as he
danced along,
he sang a happy tune.

Mum did not like it.

Dad went very red.

And all their friends just moaned and groaned, “Oh, Tyrannosaurus Ted!”

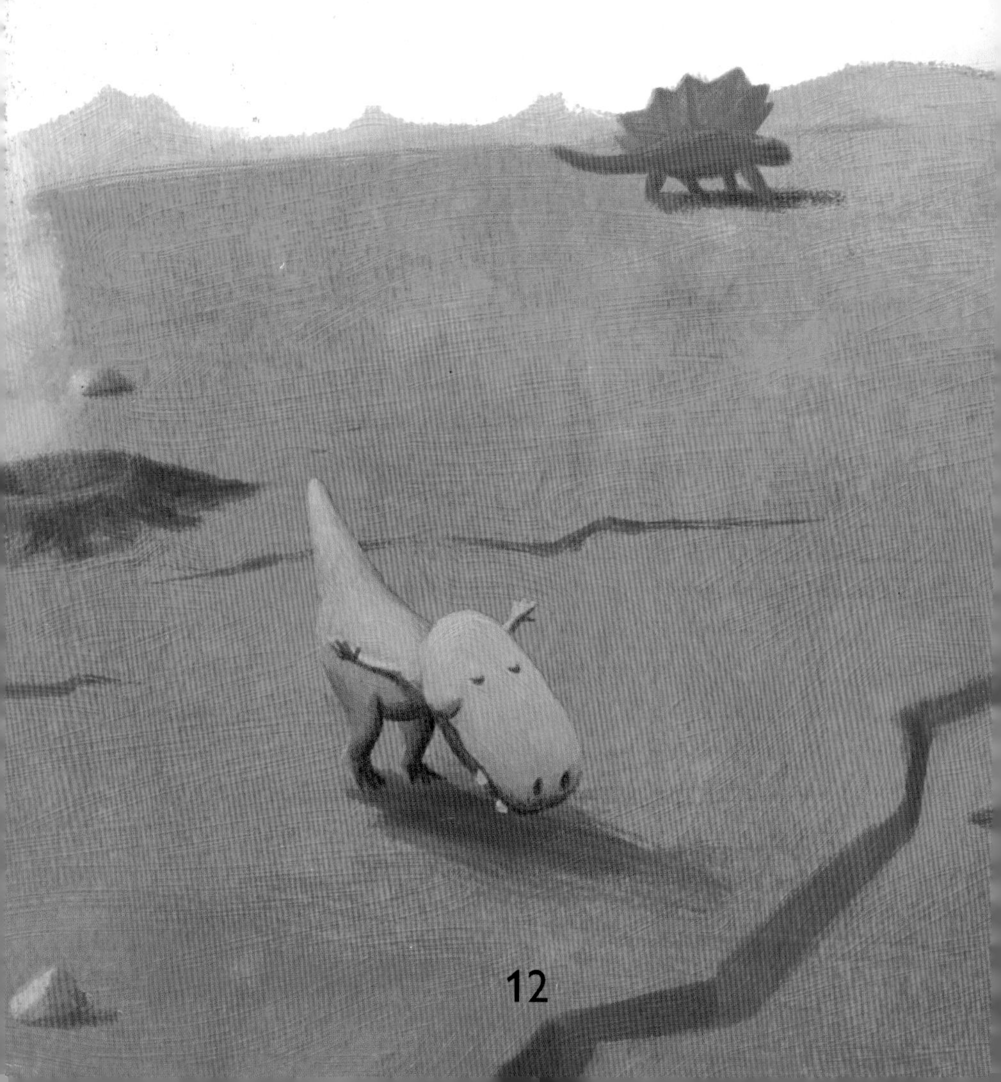

Then one day
from far away,
there came a
scary bunch.

The Giganotosaurus gang arrived,

looking for their lunch.

Mum and Dad
both trembled.

Their friends all ran away.

But Ted just danced right up and sang,

"It's a lovely sunny day."

Round and round
Ted whirled and twirled.
And then he tried a spin.

And all the time he
sang and danced,
he gave a cheeky grin.

The gang all stopped and stared at Ted. But then they tapped their feet.

"We like this tune," they all agreed. "Just listen to that beat!"

Soon all the gang were joining in, and so were Mum and Dad.

Their friends crept back
and told them both,
“Your Ted’s a clever lad.”

So now there is a hero called Tyrannosaurus Ted.

And all because he doesn't fight but likes to dance, instead.

Puzzle 1

Put these pictures in the correct order.
Now retell the story in your own words.
Is there a lesson in the story?

Puzzle 2

spin	dance
win	grin

fight	bite
play	might

crunch	lunch
bunch	gang

Find the non-rhyming word in each word box. Can you think of some words to rhyme with the odd one out?

Answers

Puzzle 1

The correct order is: 1d, 2a, 3f, 4e, 5b, 6c

Puzzle 2

The odd words out are:

dance, play, gang.

Look out for more Leapfrog Rhyme Time:

Mr Spotty's Potty
ISBN 978 0 7496 3813 3

Freddie's Fears
ISBN 978 0 7496 4382 9

Eight Enormous Elephants
ISBN 978 0 7496 4634 9

Squeaky Clean
ISBN 978 0 7496 6805 1

Felicity Floss: Tooth Fairy
ISBN 978 0 7496 6807 5

Captain Cool
ISBN 978 0 7496 6808 2

Monster Cake
ISBN 978 0 7496 6809 9

The Super Trolley Ride
ISBN 978 0 7496 6810 5

The Royal Jumble Sale
ISBN 978 0 7496 6811 2

But, Mum!
ISBN 978 0 7496 6812 9

Dan's Gran's Goat
ISBN 978 0 7496 6814 3

Lighthouse Mouse
ISBN 978 0 7496 6815 0

Big Bad Bart
ISBN 978 0 7496 6816 7

Ron's Race
ISBN 978 0 7496 6817 4

Boris the Spider
ISBN 978 0 7496 7791 6

Miss Polly's Seaside Brolly
ISBN 978 0 7496 7792 3

The Lonely Pirate
ISBN 978 0 7496 7793 0

Alfie the Sea Dog
ISBN 978 0 7496 7958 3

Red Riding Hood Rap
ISBN 978 0 7496 7959 0

Pets on Parade
ISBN 978 0 7496 7960 6

Let's Dance
ISBN 978 0 7496 7961 3

Benny and the Monster
ISBN 978 0 7496 7962 0

Bathtime Rap
ISBN 978 0 7496 7963 7

Woolly the Bully
ISBN 978 0 7496 7098 6*
ISBN 978 0 7496 7790 9

What a Frog!
ISBN 978 0 7496 7102 0*
ISBN 978 0 7496 7794 7

Juggling Joe
ISBN 978 0 7496 7103 7*
ISBN 978 0 7496 7795 4

I Wish!
ISBN 978 0 7496 7940 8*
ISBN 978 0 7496 7952 1

Raindrop Bill
ISBN 978 0 7496 7941 5*
ISBN 978 0 7496 7953 8

Sir Otto
ISBN 978 0 7496 7942 2*
ISBN 978 0 7496 7954 5

Queen Rosie
ISBN 978 0 7496 7943 9*
ISBN 978 0 7496 7955 2

Giraffe's Good Game
ISBN 978 0 7496 7944 6*
ISBN 978 0 7496 7956 9

Miss Lupin's Motorbike
ISBN 978 0 7496 7945 3*
ISBN 978 0 7496 7957 6

*hardback

For more Leapfrog books go to: www.franklinwatts.co.uk